·CLASSICS·
Illustrated. ®

Harriet Beecher Stowe
UNCLE TOM'S CABIN

essay by
Karen Karbiener, M.A., M.Phil.
Columbia University, N.Y.

ACCLAIM BOOKS
STUDY GUIDE

Uncle Tom's Cabin

art by R. Livingstone
adaptation by Evelyn Goodman
cover by Rebecca Guay

For Classics Illustrated Study Guides
computer recoloring by Twilight Graphics
editor: Madeleine Robins
assistant editor: Gregg Sanderson
design: Scott Friedlander

Dale-Chall R.L.: 7.6

ISBN 1-57840-060-0

Acclaim Books, New York, NY
Printed in the United States

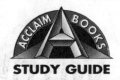

STUDY GUIDE

Uncle Tom's Cabin

by HARRIET BEECHER STOWE

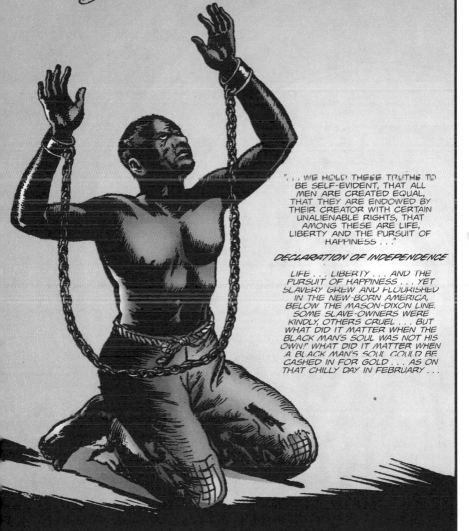

"... WE HOLD THESE TRUTHS TO BE SELF-EVIDENT, THAT ALL MEN ARE CREATED EQUAL, THAT THEY ARE ENDOWED BY THEIR CREATOR WITH CERTAIN UNALIENABLE RIGHTS, THAT AMONG THESE ARE LIFE, LIBERTY AND THE PURSUIT OF HAPPINESS ..."

DECLARATION OF INDEPENDENCE

LIFE ... LIBERTY ... AND THE PURSUIT OF HAPPINESS ... YET SLAVERY GREW AND FLOURISHED IN THE NEW-BORN AMERICA, BELOW THE MASON-DIXON LINE. SOME SLAVE-OWNERS WERE KINDLY, OTHERS CRUEL ... BUT WHAT DID IT MATTER WHEN THE BLACK MAN'S SOUL WAS NOT HIS OWN? WHAT DID IT MATTER WHEN A BLACK MAN'S SOUL COULD BE CASHED IN FOR GOLD ... AS ON THAT CHILLY DAY IN FEBRUARY ...

... ON A PLANTATION IN KENTUCKY.

I WOULDN'T EVEN CONSIDER DOING THIS, HALEY, IF I WEREN'T SO BADLY IN DEBT.

DON'T LET SELLING SLAVES BOTHER YOU, SHELBY. SLAVES AIN'T PEOPLE. I BUY 'EM UP AND SELL 'EM JUST LIKE CATTLE.

NOW, TO PICK OUT THE SLAVES I WANT. WHO'S THAT BIG FELLOW COMING OUT OF THE CABIN?

HE'S TOM ... UNCLE TOM.

SING FER US

UNCLE TOM!

"OH, I'M GOIN' TO GLORY. WON'T YOU COME ALONG WITH ME?"

YOU CAN'T THINK OF BUYING TOM. HE'S THE FINEST FELLOW I HAVE HERE ... HONEST, CAPABLE, AND A GREAT FAVORITE.

I WANT HIM, AND ... WHO'S THAT LITTLE BOY?

THAT'S ELIZA'S LITTLE BOY . . . HE'S ALL SHE HAS. IT WOULD BREAK HER HEART TO BE SEPARATED FROM HIM.

TWELVE HUNDRED DOLLARS FOR THE MAN AND BOY. IT'S GOOD MONEY. SIGN THE PAPERS, SHELBY.

HERE'S YOUR MONEY.

REMEMBER, HALEY, YOU MADE ME A CONDITION. I MUST KNOW TO WHOM YOU SELL TOM.

AS SOON AS I GET THE MONEY, I INTEND TO BUY TOM BACK.

I'LL LET YOU KNOW. HAVE BOTH SLAVES READY IN THE MORNING. I'LL BE AROUND EARLY. GOOD DAY.

PAPA, YOU AREN'T SELLING TOM?

SORRY, GEORGE, I MUST. WE'LL LOSE THE HOUSE IF I DON'T HAVE THE MONEY.

BUT ARTHUR, TO THAT HORRIBLE TRADER? OH, SLAVERY IS SO WRONG!

I GOT TO GIVE WARNING!

I'M GOING TO TRY TO REACH CANADA. IT'S SOMEWHERE WAY UP NORTH.

YOU AND DE BOY ARE LIGHT 'NOUGH COLOR TO PASS IN DE SOUTH.

INTO A MOONLESS NIGHT, ELIZA TAKES FLIGHT . . .

EARLY THE NEXT MORNING . . .

I RANG THREE TIMES FOR ELIZA. SHE HASN'T ANSWERED. WHERE IS SHE?

DAT'S WHAT I COME TO TELL YOU. SHE'S RUN OFF WIT' HER BOY.

RUN OFF?

THANK HEAVENS!

YES, MIZ SHELBY. DERE'S A MAN OUTSIDE ASKIN' FER DE BOY.

GOT AWAY, DID SHE? I'LL TRACK HER DOWN! GET MY HORSE AND HAVE TWO MEN READY. YOU COME, TOO, SHELBY.

I CAN'T. I'M GOING AWAY ON BUSINESS FOR THE DAY. SAM, ANDY, BRING MR. HALEY'S HORSE AND GO WITH HIM.

'LIZA AIN'T A FAST WALKER. THE TRADER IS APT TO CATCH UP TO HER.

WE GOT TO KEEP HIM FROM LEAVIN' SO FAST.

BOY, WE WILL! LOOKY HERE.

WHEN DAT TRADER SITS DOWN ON DIS HORSE . . .

THAT NIGHT, ELIZA, COLD AND HUNGRY, COMES TO AN INN.

IN THE INN, SHE IS RECEIVED WITHOUT TOO MANY QUESTIONS . . .

AND I'M GOING TO VISIT FRIENDS ACROSS THE RIVER FOR A FEW DAYS.

BUT THE BOATS HAVE STOPPED RUNNING. COME HERE AND LOOK.

THE EARLY SPRING THAW HAS SWOLLEN THE RIVER WITH GREAT CAKES OF FLOATING ICE!

I'VE WALKED ALL DAY, HOPING TO GET ACROSS. WHAT SHALL I DO?

THERE'S A MAN MIGHT TAKE SOME STUFF OVER LATE TONIGHT. I'LL SPEAK TO HIM. BUT IT'S A SMALL CHANCE.

ELIZA LEAPS ONTO THE FLOATING ICE.

AS ELIZA FLOUNDERS IN THE ICY WATER . . .

STEADY, NOW. I'VE GOT YOU.

A LUCKY THING YOU TUMBLED OVER NEAR SHORE. YOU'RE A BRAVE GAL. I RECKON YOU'RE RUNNING AWAY FROM A MASTER.

YES. PLEASE DON'T SEND ME BACK! PLEASE!

DON'T WORRY. I'M AGAINST SLAVERY AND I'LL FIGHT IT, ALWAYS. ME AND MY FAMILY LIVE IN THAT HOUSE. YOU CAN STAY THERE. WE'LL HELP YOU GET FURTHER AWAY.

ELIZA IS SAFE. BUT FOR HOW LONG? THE ENRAGED HALEY, UNWILLING TO LOSE HIS PREY, LOOKS UP A FRIEND OF HIS, A NOTORIOUS SLAVE-CATCHER.

I BRING THOSE SLAVES BACK DEAD OR ALIVE!

CATCH THEM ALIVE! TURN THE BOY OVER TO ME AND KEEP THE WOMAN. YOU CAN SELL HER FOR A PRETTY PENNY.

IT'S A DEAL. I GOT A WAY TO RUN 'EM DOWN!

HOURS LATER, MRS. SHELBY HEARS OF ELIZA'S AMAZING ESCAPE.

AND THERE SHE WAS, LEAPIN' AND JUMPIN' OVER THE ICE AS IF DE LAWD WAS GUIDIN' HER OVER.

I'M SO GLAD SHE ESCAPED. BUT I HATE TO THINK OF TOM IN THAT TRADER'S HANDS.

A MOMENT LATER . . .

GET IN THERE!

WAIT! I WANT TO SAY GOODBYE TO TOM.

I TELL YOU SOLEMNLY, TOM, THAT WE WILL BUY YOU BACK AS SOON AS WE HAVE THE MONEY.

I BELIEVES YOU WILL.

TOM IS SHOVED INTO THE WAGON-CART AND . . .

SHACKLES? NO, PLEASE, TOM WON'T BREAK AWAY. HE'S NEVER BEEN SHACKLED IN HIS LIFE.

I CAN'T TAKE CHANCES.

THE WAGON JOGS AWAY. THE SHELBY PLANTATION, THE ONLY HOME TOM HAS EVER KNOWN, FADES FROM VIEW.

WHERE DO I GET SOLD, MASS'R HALEY?

IN A SLAVE MARKET. I'M TAKING YOU TO ONE DOWN IN NEW ORLEANS . . . A WHOLE GANG OF YOU.

TOM FINDS A PEACEFUL BUT LONELY PERCH FOR HIMSELF ON A BALE OF COTTON...

OH! WHERE DID IT GO?

I GOT IT, LITTLE MISSY. I'LL BRING IT DOWN.

OH, THANK YOU. WHAT'S YOUR NAME? I'M EVA ST. CLARE. PAPA CALLS ME LITTLE EVA.

MY NAME IS TOM. BUT THEY USED TO CALL ME UNCLE TOM, BACK IN KENTUCK.

I'LL CALL YOU UNCLE TOM, TOO, BECAUSE I LIKE YOU

THUS BEGINS A WARM FRIENDSHIP BETWEEN THE BIG BLACK MAN AND THE LITTLE GOLDEN GIRL.

OFTEN SHE BRINGS HIM GIFTS OF CANDY AND FRUIT.

I'LL CARVE A FACE OUT OF THIS NUT.

YOU'RE SO MUCH FUN, UNCLE TOM. I WISH MY PAPA WOULD BUY YOU.

BUT, PAPA, UNCLE TOM'S SO VERY NICE.

I'D LIKE TO BUY HIM, PUSSY, BUT WE HAVE MORE HANDS ON THE PLANTATION NOW THAN WE CAN USE. THE BOAT'S STOPPING. I WONDER WHY.

THEY'RE JUST STOPPING TO TAKE IN SOME WOOD.

THERE'S UNCLE TOM HELPING.

THE WHEELS ARE STILL TURNING, PAPA. LOOK!

SUDDENLY, THE BOAT LURCHES VIOLENTLY...

DAT CHILE! SHE'S GONE OVERBOARD!

I'LL GET HER!

MY FRIEND AND I WILL DRIVE YOU ACROSS TO FREE TERRITORY.

AS THE WAGON WAS RATTLING OUT ONTO THE FROZEN ROAD . . .

THERE THEY ARE! THEY'RE TAKING THE ROAD TO SANDUSKY. QUICK, GET HORSES!

OVER THE ICY ROAD THE WAGON RACED . . . WITH THE HORSEMEN IN CLOSE PURSUIT.

THEY HAVEN'T GOT A CHANCE!

THE LITTLE PARTY SCRAMBLED UP THE LEDGE . . .

THEY'RE COMING AFTER US. I'LL STOP THEM!

I'M THEIR ENEMY. LET ME MAKE THE STAND.

WE'LL GET UP THOSE ROCKS AND SHOOT FOR IT, IF NEED BE! THIS IS FREE SOIL. THESE POOR SLAVES HAVE THEIR RIGHT TO LIVE!

THIS'LL TEACH YOU TO LET A FREE MAN BE!

HE'LL KILL US ALL! LET'S GET AWAY!

RUN, YOU COWARDS! RUN!

THE LITTLE PARTY THEN LOOKED AFTER MARK

HERE'S OUR SLAVE-CATCHER. FATE HAS BEEN KIND TO HIM.

I'D LIKE TO LEAVE HIM HANGING THERE, BUT I GUESS WE GOT TO TAKE HIM DOWN.

I'LL FIX A BANDAGE TO STOP THE BLEEDING.

YES. NO NEED TO LET HIM DIE.

IN A FEW MINUTES, MARK WAS REVIVED AND CALLING FOR HIS FRIENDS.

THERE THEY ARE, RUNNIN' FOR THEIR LIVES.

SNEAKING DOGS! LEAVING ME ALONE TO DIE. DOGS! COWARDS!

WELL, KILL ME. AREN'T YOU GOING TO KILL ME?

YOUR WOUNDS NEED LOOKING AFTER. I'VE GOT FRIENDS IN THE NEXT TOWN WHO'LL TAKE CARE OF YOU. INTO THE WAGON, EVERYONE.

AS THEY ENTER...

WHAT'S THAT?

OH! IT SOUNDS LIKE . . .

OUCH! HELP! OUCH!

. . . TOPSY! DON'T SPANK TOPSY! PLEASE, AUNT OPHELIA!

I MUST. SHE'S BEEN VERY NAUGHTY.

I DIDN' DO NUFFIN'.

LET HER UP, OPHELIA. SHE'S HAD ENOUGH.

THAT WICKED GIRL! SHE STOLE MY RIBBON AND MY GLOVES!

I DIDN' STEAL NUFFIN'. I DIDN'.

THERE! TOPSY SAID SHE DIDN'.

I'LL WAGER SHE CAN'T SAY IT TO YOUR FACE.

I CAN, TOO, MISS FEELY.

SEE!

LORDY ME! I NEVER SEEN ANYONE LIKE HER BEFORE.

WELL . . .

SAY IT, TOPSY.

I NEVER STEALED NO RIBBON AND NO GLOVES.

IF YOU DIDN'T, WHY DID I FIND THE RIBBON AND GLOVES UP YOUR SLEEVE?

'CAUSE YOU LOOKED, MISS FEELY.

I GIVE UP!

TOPSY, IF YOU WANT TO GO TO HEAVEN, TELL ME THE TRUTH.

YES'M. I WANTS TO GO TO HEBBEN. I DIDN' STEAL NUFFIN'.

MY BRACELET!

A DEBBLE MUST'VE PUT IT UP MY SLEEVE.

SHE TOOK THAT, TOO. ST. CLARE, WHAT ARE WE GOING TO DO? THRASHING DOESN'T SEEM TO HELP.

MAYBE UNCLE TOM CAN DO SOMETHING. CAN YOU, UNCLE TOM?

BUT MRS. ST. CLARE DOESN'T SEE. SPOILED, SELF-CENTERED, A VICTIM OF HER IMAGINARY AILMENTS, SHE CONSIDERS NO ONE BUT HERSELF.

LATER...

SO THIS IS UNCLE TOM. LITTLE EVA HASN'T STOPPED TALKING ABOUT YOU. I'M SURE SHE DOESN'T SPEAK SO HIGHLY OF HER OWN MOTHER.

MARIE, DON'T START THAT!

OH, MAMA!

TOM IS A FINE FELLOW.

AND HE'S TAKING CHARGE OF TOPSY. HE'S GOING TO GIVE HER A "'PORTANT" LESSON, HE SAID. I HOPE HE'S HAPPY HERE.

THAT EVENING...

THANK YOU FOR WRITIN' IT. I NEVER LEARNED HOW TO WRITE.

BUT TOM HAS LEARNED MORE. HE HAS READ THE BIBLE MANY TIMES. AND THE NEXT MORNING, AT TOPSY'S LESSON...

AND THE LORD SET DOWN THE TEN COMMANDMENTS.

IS ONE O' DEM NOT TO STEAL?

MISS FEELY READ ME ALL O' DEM. BUT DEY DON' HELP ME BE GOOD. GUESS 'CAUSE I NEVER WAS BORN.

EVERYONE WAS BORN, TOPSY.

EVA IS ALSO LOVED BY THE SLAVES. HER CHILDISH HEART OVERFLOWS WITH SYMPATHY FOR THESE BARTERED PEOPLE.

MERRY CHRISTMAS. I HAVE PRESENTS FOR EVERYONE.

BLESS YOU, LITTLE ONE.

BUT ONE DAY, THE PEACEFUL ROUTINE AT THE ST. CLARE PLANTATION IS SHATTERED.

MISSED AGAIN! YOU AIN'T PLAYIN' GOOD, LI'L EVA.

I FEEL SICK.

SUDDENLY . . .

HALP! HALP! MISSY EVA'S DAID!

SHE'S DAID!

NO, SHE'S BREATHIN', MASS'R. BUT FETCH A DOCTOR . . . QUICK!

OH, DEAR. I FEEL FAINT, MYSELF.

IT'S HER LUNGS. SHE'S A FRAIL CHILD. HER CONDITION IS SERIOUS.

EVA, MY BABY, YOU MUST LIVE.

I'LL... TRY TO, PAPA.

LORD, WE BLACKS NEVER ASKED FOR MUCH. BUT WE HAVE A BIG REQUEST NOW. SAVE LITTLE EVA. PLEASE.

'TAIN'T MUCH, MISS FEELY. I PICKED DEM OUT IN DE FIELD FOR LI'L EVA.

BLESS YOUR HEART!

UNCLE TOM, WOULD YOU LIKE TO BE BACK IN KENTUCKY WITH YOUR FAMILY?

I WOULD, LITTLE EVA. BUT I CAN'T.

BEING HERE WITH YOU IS THE NEX' BEST THING. SO YOU GOT TO GET WELL.

THAT EVENING...

PAPA, IF ANYTHING HAPPENS TO ME, WILL YOU GIVE UNCLE TOM HIS FREEDOM?

I PROMISE. BUT NOTHING WILL HAPPEN TO YOU, PUSSY.

. . . I PROMISED THAT I WOULD SET YOU FREE. I WILL SIGN THE PAPERS FOR YOU, TOMORROW.

FREE! BLESS THE LORD! I'LL GO BACK TO KENTUCK A FREE MAN.

I HEAR YOU'RE GOING TO BE SET FREE.

YES'M. MASS'R'S A KIND MAN. BUT HE'S GOIN' TO NEED LOOKIN' AFTER, MISS OPHELIA. I'SE WORRIED ABOUT HIM.

ST. CLARE! WHERE ARE YOU GOING? PLEASE DON'T DO ANYTHING RASH!

DON'T WORRY ABOUT ME.

A LITTLE LATER, IN A CAFE . . .

WHISKEY.

ME, TOO. LINE 'EM UP.

WHASH YOUR TROUBLE, FRIEN'? MINE'S WOMEN. MY BESH FRIEN' IS OUT WITH MY GAL. IF I CAN GET MY HAN'S ON 'EM . . .

THE SOT'S GLASSY GAZE SUDDENLY FOCUSES, AS . . .

THAT'S THEM! THE TRICKIN', DOUBLE-DEALIN' . . .

As ST. CLARE STEPS IN, THE OTHER MAN LUNGES.

THE NEXT DAY . . .

DEY SAY WE'RE GOIN' TO BE SOLD AT A GRAND AUCTION.

WHAT'S AN AUCTION LIKE? EVER SEE ONE, UNCLE TOM?

YES.

"THEY SELL YOUR FLESH AND BLOOD . . . YOUR BODY AND SOUL."

PLEASE BUY MY LITTLE GAL, TOO, MISTER, PLEASE . . .

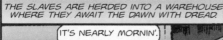

THE SLAVES ARE HERDED INTO A WAREHOUSE WHERE THEY AWAIT THE DAWN WITH DREAD.

IT'S NEARLY MORNIN'.

THE GRAND AUCTION, BIGGEST OF THE YEAR! NO ARENA IN THE DAYS OF THE ROMAN EMPERORS HELD MORE TERROR-STRICKEN SLAVES THAN THESE.

WHAT AM I BID FOR THIS FINE SPECIMEN? JUST FEEL HIS MUSCLE!

THAT SCARECROW. FIVE DOLLARS. HE'D DO TO WASH THE HORSES.

AS THE POOR SLAVE IS DRAGGED AWAY, A STIR RISES AMONG THE SPECTATORS, FOR A DYNAMIC FIGURE HAS ENTERED.

WHAT? THE BID-DING HAS BEGUN WITHOUT ME?

SIMON LEGREE!

SORRY, MR. LEGREE. WE COULDN'T WAIT ANY LONGER. BUT THE REST OF 'EM ARE STILL TO COME.

I'LL TAKE A LOOK AROUND.

LEGREE IS THE RICHEST SLAVE-OWNER IN THESE PARTS.

AND THE MEANEST. HE'S A DEVIL!

SHARP, CRUEL EYES FIX THEMSELVES ON THE TREMBLING SLAVES.

I HOPE HE DOESN'T PICK ME OUT.

HE'S PASSING US BY.

BUT SUDDENLY...

YOU, THERE! COME OUT!

A REVOLTING HORROR SWEEPS OVER TOM AS HE NEARS THE SLAVE-TRADER.

OPEN YOUR MOUTH. LET ME SEE YOUR TEETH.

PRETTY STRONG. I NEED 'EM STRONG FOR MY KIND OF WORK. I'LL BID FOR THIS ONE.

AND TOM'S FATE IS DECIDED. HE IS HUDDLED WITH OTHER NEWLY-PURCHASED SLAVES ON A SMALL, MEAN BOAT POINTED TOWARD LEGREE'S RED RIVER COTTON PLANTATION.

I WON'T WORK FOR THAT MAN! I'M GOING TO KILL MYSELF!

NO ONE MUST GIVE WAY LIKE THAT. WE GOT TO HAVE FAITH -- FAITH IN THE LORD, WHO WILL TAKE CARE OF HIS CHILLEN. CHEER UP, EVERYONE. MAYBE A SONG WILL HELP.

STOP THAT! I'LL HAVE NONE O' YER BAWLING, PRAYING, SINGING NIGGERS ON MY PLACE. I SAW WHO STARTED THIS AND I'LL TAKE CARE OF HIM!

MY FIST GOT AS HARD AS IRON KNOCKING DOWN NIGGERS!

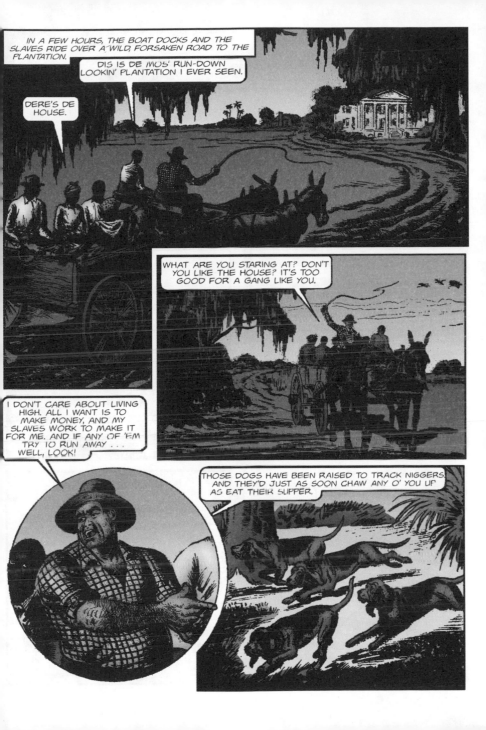

A FEW DAYS LATER AT THE SHELBY PLANTATION . . .

IT'S FROM MISS OPHELIA. SHE WRITES THAT TOM WAS SOLD TO A CRUEL MASTER. WE MUST BUY TOM BACK.

CAN'T WE, FATHER?

THAT'S IMPOSSIBLE. I HAVE MORE NOTES COMING DUE.

POOR UNCLE TOM. POOR AUNT CHLOE. SHE'LL FEEL BADLY AT TOM'S PLIGHT.

I BEEN THINKIN' ABOUT A WAY TO RAISE MONEY EVER SINCE I HEARED ABOUT DE PASTRY SHOP IN DE NEX' TOWN.

PASTRY SHOP?

DEY NEED SONEONE TO MAKE CAKES AND PIES. IF YOU HIRED ME OUT TO DEM, MY WAGES COULD GO TO BUYIN' BACK TOM.

THEY SHALL, CHLOE.

I KNOW IT WILL TAKE AT LEAST TWO OR THREE YEARS. BUT DAT'S BETTER'N NOTHIN'

IT WONT TAKE THAT LONG. I SHALL ADD SOME MONEY TO WHAT YOU MAKE.

ON SIMON LEGREE'S PLANTATION, THE SLAVES ARE AT WORK FROM EARLY DAWN TO THE LAST RAY OF LIGHT... DAY AFTER DAY AFTER DAY.

FASTER! YOU LAZY BLACK!

I'M DOIN' MY FASTES'.

THAT TOM'S A FIRST-CLASS HAND. I GOT HIM PICKED OUT TO BE AN OVERSEER.

ONE DAY, AT THE WEIGHING IN... A ROUTINE BUSINESS THAT FOLLOWS THE PICKING...

YOU'RE A POUND SHORT, YOU GOOD-FOR-NOTHING!

HE'LL KILL ME, UNCLE TOM. I HAVEN'T ENOUGH!.

DON'T YOU WORRY, EMMELINE. I GOT MORE'N ENOUGH. TAKE SOME OF MINE.

YOU ARE GOOD, UNCLE TOM.

HE'S 'BOUT THE BESTEST I EVER SEEN.

BUT...

THE BEATING LEAVES TOM GROANING, BLEEDING, HELPLESS . . .

WATER... WATER...

SOFT FOOTSTEPS REACH HIS EARS . . .

WHO'S THERE? OH, FOR THE LORD'S MERCY, PLEASE GIVE ME WATER.

IT'S CASSY AND ME.

POOR UNCLE TOM.

THE BEASTS! LEAVING YOU IN THIS SHED! WE HAD A TIME FINDING YOU.

WE HAVE A PLAN THAT WILL GET US AWAY FROM HERE. MEET US BACK OF THE SHED TOMORROW NIGHT.

THE NEXT MORNING . . .

YOU LEFT HIM IN THE SHED? GET HIM! HE'LL GROVEL ON HIS KNEES AND BEG MY PARDON!

NOW WHO'S RIGHT? GET DOWN ON YOUR KNEES AND TELL ME I'M RIGHT!

NO. I CAN'T... BECAUSE YOU'RE NOT RIGHT.

THE FURIOUS LEGREE IS ABOUT TO STRIKE HIM AGAIN. THEN HE CHANGES HIS MIND, FOR HE NEEDS TOM TO WORK IN THE FIELDS. BUT HE VOWS THAT HE IS NOT DONE WITH THE SLAVE YET.

ANOTHER TOILING DAY. THEN AT MIDNIGHT...

HOW CAN YOU RUN AWAY? THOSE BLOOD DOGS'LL TRAIL YOU.

WE'LL PUT THEM ON THE SWAMP TRAIL, WHILE WE HIDE IN THE ATTIC. LEGREE THINKS THE ATTIC IS HAUNTED. HE'LL NEVER LOOK THERE.

WHEN THEY'RE THROUGH LOOKIN'. WE'LL GET AWAY TO THE RED RIVER BOAT. WE GOT ENOUGH MONEY FOR PASSAGE.

WE CAN PASS AS WHITES, AND WE'LL SAY YOU ARE OUR SERVANT, UNCLE TOM.

NO, I'M TOO OLD FOR RUNNIN' AWAY. THERE'S NO USE MY TRYIN', NOW BUT I'LL KEEP YOUR SECRET AND I HOPE THE LORD WILL KEEP YOU SAFE.

THE OLD DEVIL. READY, CASSY?

HERE IT GOES!

WHO'S BACK THERE? WHO MADE THAT NOISE?

HE DASHES TO THE BACK DOOR, AS THE TWO SHADOWY FIGURES FLEE . . .

YOU! COME BACK HERE! SAMBO! QUIMBO! ALL HANDS!

THERE'S TWO RUNAWAYS MAKING FOR THE SWAMPS. FIVE DOLLARS TO ANY NIGGER WHO CATCHES THEM. TURN OUT THE DOGS! TIGER, FURY, ALL OF THEM!

THE SAVAGE HUNT IS UNDER WAY. THE SHOUTING OF MEN BLENDS WITH THE WILD YELPS OF THE BEASTS.

IT WON'T BE EASY TO TRACK 'EM. THE SCENT OF HUMANS DON'T LAST IN THE WATER

WE GOT TO CATCH 'EM!

AS THE PREY-MAD PARTY PLUNGES INTO THE SWAMP, THE RUNAWAY MAKE THEIR WAY OUT AND BACK INTO AN EMPTIED HOUSE.

WE'LL HAVE TO HIDE HERE TILL THE HUNT DIES DOWN. LEGREE WILL BE RAISING HEAVEN AND EARTH SEARCHING FOR US

AT EARLY DAWN, THE SLAVE-HUNTERS RETURN.

IT'S EMMELINE AND CASSY WHO GOT AWAY. THEY AIN'T IN THEIR ROOM.

WE'LL GO OUT AGAIN FOR THEM AS SOON AS THE DOGS GET RESTED.

AT THE END OF THAT DAY...

THEY'RE BACK AGAIN.

GUESS THEY DIDN'T FIND US.

AFTER ANOTHER DAY OF DESPERATE HUNTING...

NO USE. THEY MUST'VE GOT THROUGH THE SWAMPS BY NOW.

IT'S THE FIRST TIME ANY OF THOSE DEVILS GOT AWAY FROM ME!

FURY AT HIS FAILURE DRIVES LEGREE TO HARD DRINK. SUDDENLY...

I KNOW WHO'S AT THE BOTTOM OF THEIR ESCAPE. IT'S THAT OLD CUSS, TOM HE'LL KNOW WHERE THEY ARE! GET HIM!

BEFORE SAMBO AND QUIMBO START OUT, A GUST OF WIND BLOWS THE DOOR OPEN.

GHOSTS! THEY'VE COME BACK!

G-GHOSTS?

THE . . . THE DOOR MUST'VE BLOWN OPEN.

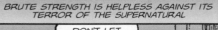

BRUTE STRENGTH IS HELPLESS AGAINST ITS TERROR OF THE SUPERNATURAL

DON'T LET THEM GET ME!

OUT THE OTHER DOOR GLIDE THE 'GHOSTS', CHUCKLING TO THEMSELVES.

SOON AS WE GET FAR ENOUGH AWAY, EMMELINE, WE'LL BURY THE SHEETS.

THEY'LL THINK IT WAS GHOSTS FOR THE REST OF THEIR LIVES.

BUT . . .

THE FOLLOWING MORNING, A SOBERED BUT VIOLENT LEGREE QUESTIONS TOM.

HOW DID THOSE GALS ESCAPE? WHERE DID THEY GO? TELL ME, OR I'LL KILL YOU!

YOU'LL HAVE TO KILL ME, THEN.

THUS CLOSES THE STORY OF UNCLE TOM. DEATH ENDS THE LIFE OF TROUBLE AND TOIL. THE SLAVE IS FREE AT LAST.

POOR UNCLE TOM'S LIFE IS OVER, BUT IT HAS LEFT A VIVID IMPRINT. I'M GLAD YOU BROUGHT THE BODY HOME. TOM WOULD HAVE WANTED TO BE BURIED HERE.

THERE'S SOMETHING MORE UNCLE TOM WOULD HAVE WANTED, MOTHER

LATER . . .

GOOD, MOTHER. GOOD.

WHEN UNCLE TOM DIED, I MADE UP MY MIND NEVER TO OWN ANY MORE SLAVES. I HAVE A CERTIFICATE OF FREEDOM FOR EACH ONE OF YOU.

FREE! WE ARE FREE! BLESS YOU! THE LORD BLESS YOU!

I WISH ALL SLAVES COULD BE AS LUCKY AS US!

SOMEDAY, THEY'LL ALL BE FREE. NO RACE OR RELIGION ON THE FACE OF THE EARTH WAS MEANT TO ENSLAVE ANOTHER.

THE END

UNCLE TOM'S CABIN
HARRIET BEECHER STOWE

"So you're the little woman who made this great war," President Abraham Lincoln on meeting Harriet Beecher Stowe. The war, of course, was the American Civil War. Even Stowe herself was baffled by the influence and repercussions of *Uncle Tom's Cabin*; her confusion is apparent in her comment regarding the book late in life, when she declared "God wrote it." The daughter of Reverend Lyman Beecher, sister to six ministers, and married to the Reverend Calvin Stowe, Harriet had been brought up to seek answers in religion, and to ascribe power to men. But it really was this petite, unassuming woman who sat at a desk in the corner of her dining room and, amidst the cares and distractions of her duties as wife and mother, wrote one of the most influential and discussed books in American history.

Harriet Beecher Stowe was raised in Connecticut, the seventh child of eight who survived the death of Lyman Beecher's first wife, Roxana. Harriet's father was a strict Calvinist who often lectured his children regarding the horrifying penalties of their sins. Additionally, he was typical of his generation in his discriminatory attitude towards women; though he recognized seven-year-old Harriet as a genius, he added that he wished she had been a boy.

Despite the intellectual and educational limitations imposed on her by her gender, Harriet read voraciously and began to see some of her writings published in magazines by the age of twenty-three. She continued writing after she married a poor minister and had seven children, to supplement the household income. *Uncle Tom's Cabin*, her first longer work, was originally written in nine months of installments for a magazine called *The National Era*. When the sketches were published in book form the next year, Harriet earned enough in royalties to lift her family out of poverty, and to enable her to pursue her literary career.

Stowe first became interested in the issue of slavery when she and her family moved to Cincinnati in 1832; there and in Kentucky, where she visited slaveholding friends, she was introduced to the African race and the problems of the "patriarchal institution." But she was not compelled to write on the subject until 1850, when she and her family moved to Brunswick, Maine. The excitement over the Fugitive Slave Law

was then at its height; the terror and despair it caused affected Stowe strongly. Pondering the stories she read in anti-slavery magazines and drawing upon her own experiences, the busy wife and mother began to write the book that she claimed "insisted upon getting itself into being, and would take no denial."

Stowe wrote many other novels after *Uncle Tom's Cabin,* though none approached that book's popularity. To further the antislavery cause, she wrote her second novel,

A Book with a Rep

It's best to admit up front that *Uncle Tom's Cabin* carries a lot of baggage with it: the name conjures up Victorian sentimentality and the worst kind of Victorian racism. To appreciate *Uncle Tom's Cabin* you have to look past its reputation—and try to read it, not as a student from the 1990s, but as a reader of the 1850s, when the world was a *very* different place.

Extreme sentimentality and religiousness aren't exactly ingredients of a modern-day bestseller (imagine a sappy Stephen King novel or a churchgoing Jackie Collins heroine...). Today, readers of *Uncle Tom's Cabin* may have trouble relating to the story's melodramatic or religious moments, such as those showcasing Eva's angelic goodness or Tom's unshaken faith in God's grace. But it is important to remember that the appeal of such emotions and feelings were very powerful, not only for Stowe personally but for most of her 19th century American audience. Indeed, many other popular novels of the time, such as *Moby Dick* (1850) and *The Scarlet Letter* (1851), also contain scenes that are melodramatic or religiously didactic. So, just as we might hear and enjoy a song from the 1970s even if we don't sympathize with its message, we can appreciate the strong emotional and religious sentiments motivating Stowe's characters,

though we might not share these feelings. To be fully understood and respected, artists—as diverse as Led Zeppelin and Harriet Beecher Stowe—should be placed in the context of their time, even though their work is great in and of itself.

What might be harder to get past than the novel's melodrama or piety is what seems to be its demeaning tone towards African-Americans. Tom's behavior, and especially his language, is humbler and simpler than that of the white characters. His accent, grammatical errors, and vocabulary make him seem more like a stereotype than a real person (and supporting characters of color may seem even more caricatured). But in representing Tom this way, Stowe was not intentionally racist. Instead, she worked within her limited understanding of African-Americans to represent them as she thought they acted and spoke. Her concern for accuracy in portraying black American English can be seen in the care and consistency with which she created Tom's speech; studies have shown that she made meticulous revisions to Tom's language between the serial and book versions of *Uncle Tom's Cabin.* Stowe's sensitivity to issues of race might not be as apparent to us today, but her intentions in writing an anti-slavery novel are clearly good ones.

Dred: A Tale of the Great Dismal Swamp; she also wrote several books using New England themes and color, such as *The Pearl of Orr's Island* and *Oldtown Folks*. With the freedom given her from book royalties and an "empty nest" of a home, Stowe traveled to Europe three times and was even honored by Queen Victoria. Towards the end of her life, Stowe realized that her mental capacities were failing. "And now I rest me, like a moored boat, rising and falling on the water, with loosened cordage and flapping sail," she wrote to her doctor in 1893. She died peacefully three years later, surrounded by her large family and the material comforts she had never known in her youth.

Context

When Harriet Beecher Stowe sat down to write *Uncle Tom's Cabin* in the mid-19th century, slavery was a long-standing and profitable international institution. Africans had been imported into Europe for forced labor since Roman times. The Muslim world also bought and sold African slaves, although without distinguishing between black and white. The first black Africans to be transported to North America were brought to what is now Virginia by Dutch traders in 1619, a year before the Pilgrim Fathers arrived. With the rise of the American plantation economy in the 18th century, slaves became the basis of a substantial industry, and the numbers of black Africans shipped to America rose sharply. Stowe herself had visited many slave plantations, and even numbered slave holders among her family and friends.

The fact that slavery was legal, however, does not mean that people were oblivious to its wrongs. After all, only nine years after *Uncle Tom's Cabin* appeared as a serial in a magazine, the United States would erupt in civil war over the issue. Already there were signs that the opinions concerning slavery would divide the nation. After the American Revolution, all states north of Maryland took steps toward the abolition of slavery, and the French revolutionary government abolished it in 1794 throughout the French colonies; indeed, black Africans in France had already received their civil rights.

But in 1850, the United States Congress enacted a law that outraged those who fought for slavery's abolition: the Fugitive Slave Law. Citizens in the free states had always been required by the Constitution to return runaway slaves; with the passing of the new law, common legal safeguards such as a judicial hearing or a jury trial were no longer parts of the process. The task of returning fugitive slaves was taken out of the hands of the courts and turned over to federal commissioners. All the pursuing slave holder or his agent had to do was to present proof of ownership to the commissioner, who had the power to declare the runaway free or to turn him over to the supposed owner. A commissioner was paid five dollars if he decided that a person was not a slave, and ten dollars if he was. The commissioner's ruling was final; no appeal could be made in or out of the courts. Supposedly, the reason that these fees were different was because the commissioner would have to file more papers to return a slave rather than free him. But those fighting against slavery believed that the differing payments would tempt commissioners to rule against alleged fugitives in doubtful cases. The Fugitive Slave Act not only made it more difficult for runaway slaves to escape; it also posed a potential threat to the lives and liberty of free blacks.

Shocked and dismayed by the descriptions of the operation of the Fugitive Slave Law, spurred on by similarly outraged friends and fans, Stowe was inspired to write one of the 19th century's most powerful indictments against the practice of slavery. The incredible popularity of *Uncle Tom's Cabin* attested to the timeliness and relevance of her message. Though slavery was not prohibited in America until the Thirteenth Amendment to the United States Constitution was passed in 1865, Stowe's masterpiece of 1852 helped America recognize the importance—and the inevitability—of emancipation in the "home of the free."

The Characters

Tom: The tragic hero of Stowe's novel, Tom is an idealized, Christ-like figure: he sustains himself and others through his faith in God, submits without protest to cruelty and mistreatment, and suffers a horrible death for the sake of those he loves. To the modern reader, Tom appears excessively meek from the beginning when, unlike Eliza, he is willing to be separated from his family and remain obedient to his master. Yet the title of the book reminds us that Tom's foremost concern through all his experiences is his reunion with his wife and children in "Uncle Tom's cabin"—the closest thing to a "home" that he has ever known.

Stowe gave Tom qualities which are now representative of degrading racial stereotypes, such as his speech patterns and his humble simplicity. It is also evident, however, that she modeled him after her idea of a true and perfect Christian. Indeed, Stowe

ALL THESE PEOPLE GOIN' TO HOMES OF THEIR OWN. ALL OF THEM BUT THE BLACK MAN. HE AIN'T GOT NO HOME. WHERE AM I GOIN'? WHERE?

WHERE CAN A SLAVE IN THE SOUTH REST HIS WEARY HEAD? TOM WONDERS ABOUT HIS FUTURE, LITTLE AWARE THAT A CRISIS IN HIS LIFE IS FAST APPROACHING.

ice admitted that one of the actual people who inspired the character of Tom was the Reverend Josiah Henson. An escaped slave, this kindly, good-humored minister helped other slaves find freedom; the second edition of his autobiography contained an introduction written by Stowe.

Mr. Shelby: Tom's first master, this Kentucky plantation owner is forced by economic pressure to sell Eliza's son Harry and Tom, despite his own attachment to his slaves, the protests of Mrs. Shelby, and the affection of their son George. Mr. Shelby probably thinks of himself as a kindly master; he does not physically mistreat his slaves, and he shows genuine affection for Tom, Eliza, and Harry. But he is also a businessman who is willing to put a price on people that he cares for— and in this way, he represents the hardened attitude of many of the slave owners of Stowe's day. Notably, Shelby is not present to say goodbye to Tom; it is his wife who offers Tom reassurance of his eventual return, and supports Eliza's decision to run away. Furthermore, Shelby never delivers on his promise to buy Tom back. At the end, his son George arrives to correct his father's wrongs; though his intentions are good, he is too late to save Tom from a terrible fate.

Eliza: Though Tom is certainly the central character of *Uncle Tom's Cabin*, the story of Eliza's successful flight to freedom in Canada forms an important subplot. A light-skinned, beautiful slave on the Shelby plantation, Eliza is warned that her son Harry has been sold to a slave trader. Eliza is justified in her terror of being separated from her own child; in Stowe's day, many slave owners and slave traders thought nothing of separating families.

ELIZA LEAPS ONTO THE FLOATING ICE.

Eliza and Harry's adventures as they escaped from slavery provide *Uncle Tom's Cabin* with some of its most exciting moments. Indeed, perhaps the most memorable passage in the novel is that of Eliza clutching her child while crossing the turbulent, ice-choked Ohio River, enslavement her sure fate on one riverbank and freedom promised by the other. In the last chapter of *Uncle Tom's Cabin*, Stowe claimed that this incident was based on an actual happening; several versions of this alleged incident were reported in abolitionist periodicals of her day.

Haley: This crude slave dealer purchases Tom, Eliza, and her son from Mr. Shelby, with the intention of bringing them to a New Orleans slave market. When Eliza and her child ran away from him, Haley hires an even more cruel slave catcher to retrieve them. But Haley himself is not the story's villain. He is simply a middleman, a morally ambiguous businessman whose position has been created by the greediness and cruelty of others. Though his dress, speech, and mannerisms make him seem the most despicable, it is the "decent" man—the well-dressed, intelligent, and cultivated gentleman, like Augustine St. Clare—who is the root cause of slavery's depravity.

Augustine St. Clare: Tom's kindest master, St. Clare is a slave owner who readily admits and recognizes that slavery is wrong. Born in Louisiana, St. Clare also spent time in Vermont as a youth, so he is familiar with the differing ideas and attitudes of the South and the North concerning this issue. His divided stance on this issue is echoed in the personalities of the two women he lives with: his southern-bred wife Marie, who is vain, sickly, and closed-minded, and his sister Ophelia from Vermont, who is righteous according to old Calvinistic

standards, but also good-hearted and sympathetic.

Divided within, St. Clare has let go of his decision-making authority as head of the family. Sometimes this is for the best, as in his easy going attitude concerning his daughter's interracial friendships with his slaves; other times it is for the worst,

as when he simply puts up with wife's complaints and prejudiced opinions. Ultimately, his in-between position brings about his own death when he gets in the middle of a barroom brawl and is fatally stabbed. And St. Clare's inability to make a decision to the very end, as he puts off signing Tom's slavery release forms, continues to damage and destroy the lives of others even after his own death.

Evangeline St. Clare: With her "long, golden brown hair that floated like a cloud" and "the deep spiritual gravity of her violet blue eyes," Eva is the representative of perfect innocence in *Uncle Tom's Cabin*. She might even be called Tom's guardian angel (note that "angel" is positioned in the middle of her name); though he rescues her when she falls off the ferryboat bound for New Orleans, she "saves" him by getting her father to buy Tom and bring him to a happy, stable home. Accordingly, when the fragile little girl dies, the power of her "religion of love" is lifted from the St. Clare plantation: her father is soon killed, the great house is sold, and Tom is sold to his last and cruelest owner, Simon Legree.

Topsy: The most important black character introduced in the New Orleans plantation scenes of *Uncle Tom's Cabin*, Topsy is a little girl who seems, at first, to provide some comic relief to the novel. But though she often sounds funny, as when she explains how she was born, her humor hides a need of love and closeness that becomes evident when Eva dies.

When we first meet Topsy, she doesn't seem to know or to care about the difference between right and wrong, merrily denying that she stole

Ophelia's ribbon and gloves even after being caught in the act. Ophelia's attempts to correct Topsy's behavior with physical punishment are ineffective, much like the beatings given to Uncle Tom and others throughout the book.

Simon Legree: Tom's third owner, Simon Legree, is viciousness incarnate, and Stowe's attempt to show the state of slavery at its worst. The bachelor owner of the profitable but run-down Red River plantation in Louisiana, Legree rules over his slaves with an iron fist, and has even taught two of them—Sambo and Quimbo—to turn against their fellow sufferers. Despite his physical strength, Legree has no power to bend Tom's will; and though Legree eventually kills Tom, he is never able to destroy his spirit.

Though Legree appears to be a man without heart

or soul, we do learn about some of the fears and weaknesses lurking behind his sneer. For one, he is terrified of the supernatural, as is evident from his reaction to Emmeline's and Cassy's ghost impression. In Stowe's book, the detail emerges that Legree had once killed a black woman in the attic, and that house slaves claimed to hear moans from there. Perhaps Legree's fear of ghosts is a hint of submerged feelings of guilt.

Cassy: One of Simon Legree's house slaves, Cassy is the beautiful, well-educated daughter of a white man and his almost-white slave. Despite her cultivated manners and pale skin, Cassy has been treated as something less than human, simply due to her mother's bloodline; Stowe's book details more of Cassy's experiences as mistress and slave to various owners before she was sold to Legree. Along with Emmeline, a pretty young mulatto woman who was bought by Legree at the same time as Tom, Cassy plans a clever escape from the Red River plantation which involves outwitting their cruel master. Serving as their protector, Tom refuses to give Legree details of their plan. The price of their freedom turns out to be Tom's demise.

In writing *Uncle Tom's Cabin,* Stowe followed a practice often used by 19th-century novelists—and even modern TV writers—to keep audiences involved: she alternated between the adventures of two different groups of characters. In doing so, Stowe also provided her readers with a broader and more varied picture of society, and expanded the emotional appeal of her book.

The two stories have the same beginning, on the Shelby plantation in Kentucky. Tom, an intelligent black man in early middle age, is sold to a slave trader, and taken further south to a slave market. His experiences form the main plot of *Uncle Tom's Cabin,* and introduce us to the world of slavery. In the second plot, one of Tom's fellow slaves serves as the central figure: Eliza, a light-skinned, beautiful mother of an adorable little boy. Fleeing from the same slave trader who bought Tom, Eliza and her family head north to Canada and are helped by abolitionist enthusiasts like those who formed part of the Underground Railway. Though Tom's saga becomes the focus of the book, the two different stories are developed with an almost architectural balance of details: for example,

the fate of a dark-skinned African such as Tom versus that of the lighter Eliza, the consequences of allowing oneself to be separated from one's family compared to fighting to keep it together, and the results of heading south versus north. In the end, we see juxtaposed the refuge found by Eliza and her family in free Ontario and Tom's solitary misery in Louisiana.

What can a slave really consider as his or her "home?" For both Tom and Eliza, their families serve as the bases of their lives. But Tom, in his humble obedience, obeys his orders and leaves his wife and children. Eliza's maternal instinct is much more powerful than her ties to her master; in Stowe's book, we learn that Eliza had two other children that had died. The thought of losing her precious Harry leads her to turn against all those who have loved and supported her. Her odds for gaining her freedom in Canada seem as remote as her chance of making it across the half-frozen Ohio River on foot. She manages, however, to do both. And even after ruthless slave catchers have chased her with the intention to kill, she demonstrates her own decency by nursing one of her wounded pursuers. This act of Christian charity proves her moral superiority even over those on the side of "the law."

Meanwhile, Tom's faith has also served him well. On the boat down the New Orleans slave market, Haley notices Tom's ability to keep slaves content and quiet with prayers and hymns; he therefore grants Tom some freedom to walk about. And it is Tom's Christian goodness that allows him to bond with the angelic Eva St. Clare.

I'LL CALL YOU UNCLE TOM, TOO, BECAUSE I LIKE YOU

THUS BEGINS A WARM FRIENDSHIP BETWEEN THE BIG BLACK MAN AND THE LITTLE GOLDEN GIRL

The large black man and the delicate, pale little girl may be worlds apart in terms of their upbringing, education, and place in society, but they are both idealized, self-sacrificing figures—like Christ, whose life and writings are often discussed by Eva and Tom. Stowe shows in their friendship the basic human ability to overcome prejudice, and to forget all distinctions of race, sex, and social status. The pair becomes not only physically inseparable, but emotionally tied; and when it becomes apparent that a person as good and pure as Eva cannot survive in an environment that allows such atrocities as slavery, we know that gentle Tom is also in trouble.

EVA, MY BABY, YOU MUST LIVE.

I'LL... TRY TO, PAPA.

The years Tom spends on the St. Clare plantation form the central chapters of *Uncle Tom's Cabin*, and provide Tom with his happiest moments spent away from his family. This is largely due to the kindness and fair treatment of his master, Augustine St. Clare. A dashing, charismatic figure, St. Clare has traveled widely in both the northern and southern regions of the United States. Raised in Vermont, he understands and appreciates the arguments of abolitionists; and while he still owns slaves, he treats them almost like members of his family. Tom learns to read under St. Clare's care, and Topsy receives the love and security of a stable home for the first time in her life. St. Clare's benevolence and open-mindedness have clearly been passed on to his daughter. Their relationship is reciprocal and perfectly balanced: while St. Clare nurtures the goodness in his child, Eva helps preserve her father's faith in humanity. That is why when Eva dies, St. Clare is also drained of his lifeblood. A lost man, he tries to find consolation outside of his home—a significant and foreboding act in a book about the importance of family.

We might wonder why Eva remains the most important female in St. Clare's life, especially considering that he lives with two others: his wife Marie, and his sister Ophelia from Vermont. Couldn't these women hold the St. Clare family together, or at least keep St. Clare from destroying himself? Stowe's book makes clear that Marie and Ophelia serve such opposing ideals that life with both of them is a struggle, or a series of compromises, for the all-too-easygoing St. Clare. Marie is the stereotypical southern belle: beautiful, but selfish, demanding, and prejudiced. Ophelia is a representative of Puritan New England and its rigid rules of conduct; though she learns about love and sympathy from Eva and Tom, she has a natural hardness about her. In creating these two characters, Stowe suggests that there were problems with the attitudes and opinions of both the southerners and the northerners in regards to the slavery issue: while southerners were guilty of supporting and maintaining the institution, those from the north often hid behind a cloak of religion-inspired righteousness.

It seems fitting, then, that the villainous slave driver Simon Legree was also born and raised in Vermont. In his character, Stowe has combined stereotypes of northern and southern behavior, and created a hideous mess: here we have a man who chooses to run his southern plantation with Yankee efficiency and discipline. Tom certainly possesses exceptional character, and has built his inner strength with Eva's help; but he may have met his match in his last and worst owner, who seems to be as powerful physically as Tom is spiritually. Legree himself certainly recognizes the challenge presented by Tom, and does everything he can to weaken

Tom's soul: for example, Legree prohibits Tom from singing and praying, and often tries to get Tom to beg for mercy.

Legree thrives on the image of himself as a hardened, profit-driven plantation owner.

But is the bachelor as tough as he claims to be? In her book, Stowe drops several hints that Legree does have his weaknesses. For one, he has a fondness for keeping pretty African women as house slaves; when his two favorites, Emmeline and Cassy, run away, he is infuriated to the point that he could—and does—commit murder. He does, then, crave human companionship, and may even be susceptible to feelings of love. Legree is also very superstitious, as he demonstrates in Emmeline's and Cassy's ghost enactment scene. No living man can awaken fear in Legree's heart, and yet he is terrified of spirits. Perhaps this signifies that Legree is in fact "haunted" in some way, by his past, his actions, or his own guilt.

Legree's relentless beatings finally prove to be too much for Tom, who dies in a pool of his own blood. But though Tom's body is broken, his spirit lives on. George Shelby, the son of Tom's original owner, has ome to Legree's plantation to keep his father's promise of buying Tom back. Can the next generation make up for the sins of the forefathers? It seems so, in some ways at least: horrified by Tom's death, George is inspired to release all of his slaves. Thus, though Tom himself is never given the liberty he longed for, his death helps grant freedom to his wife, children, and indeed the "human family" of both the novel and 19th century America.

Equality

What truths or insights does *Uncle Tom's Cabin* reveal? To the original readers it was a strong statement concerning the wrongs of slavery and the need to bring an end to a vicious and inhumane practice. After emancipation was accomplished, readers found broader applications of Stowe's original theme, reading the book as a general indictment of man's inhumanity to man. While some of the attitudes expressed in *Uncle Tom's Cabin* seem to reinforce stereotypes and the idea of racial inequality, the book is still a powerful argument for the full and equal brotherhood of all men. For example, though Tom acts subserviently and accepts his fate as a slave, he proves that he is worthy of equal treatment by the St. Clare family when he saves Eva's life.

Tom knows, too, that both black and white peoples will "go to glory" together, after death. Hoping to excite our horror and indignation, Stowe paints ugly portraits of characters who fight against recognizing the equality of all races, like Haley and Simon Legree; those who are truly nondiscriminatory, like Eva or young George Shelby, are described in glowing and almost angelic terms. Eliciting our sympathy for oppressed people, appealing to our dignity and morality, and evoking our religious sensibility, *Uncle Tom's Cabin* convinces us that ultimately there is only one race: the human race.

SOMEDAY, THEY'LL ALL BE FREE. NO RACE OR RELIGION ON THE FACE OF THE EARTH WAS MEANT TO ENSLAVE ANOTHER.

THE END

Family

Stowe isn't just concerned with pointing out the importance of our broader human family; she also shows how crucial and central the family is for our happiness, well-being, and moral centeredness. In *Uncle Tom's Cabin*, any time a family is lacking or falling apart, trouble is sure to be brewing. This starts when Tom is separated from his wife and children; is evident again when we meet Topsy, the amoral little girl who "never had a mammy or pappy"; is demonstrated when Eva St. Clare dies; and is seen again in the evil character of the bachelor, Simon Legree. On the other hand, a happy ending comes to Eliza, who risks everything to keep her family together. Even the title *Uncle Tom's Cabin* was chosen with family in mind: it was in his cabin, with his wife and children, that Tom was most content, and it is here that he wishes to return until the very end.

though he hurts Tom physically, he never touches or harms Tom's most valuable possession: his soul. The example of Topsy serves well here, too. Being beaten by Ophelia with a hairbrush has no effect on Topsy's lies and stealing. But when Tom treats the orphan with kindness and teaches her to sing, people begin to see Topsy's true gentleness and goodness.

Non-Violence

Another theme that might be distilled from Stowe's novel is the superiority of peaceful problem-solving over violence and force. Her idea anticipates Ghandi's and Martin Luther King Jr.'s philosophy of non-violence; indeed, some people have compared the martyrdom of Tom to King's death in 1968. Tom's willingness to submit to mistreatment and beatings, especially those of his murderer, Simon Legree, is sometimes read as a weakness in his character, or as Stowe's use of a racial stereotype. But how does Legree's use of force really work to his benefit, or accomplish anything? Legree receives no information about Emmeline and Cassy's escape, and he has killed one of his finest workers—an overseer of the plantation, no less. And

Woman's Power

Stowe never became a radical feminist like her sister, Isabella Beecher Hooker. But she had tremendous faith in the power of women, and one of the themes she incorporated into *Uncle Tom's Cabin* was women's ability to revolutionize a man's world. Stowe accepted as valid many of the stereotypes assigned to male and female: the "masculine sphere" was the authoritative, money-making realm, and the "feminine sphere" was a world of hope, charity, mercy, and self-sacrifice. In her opinion, the feminine attributes were the most important because they placed the welfare of the group over the individual, and replaced the ideas of control and discipline with love and nurture. Women weren't only the moral superiors of man, they were pirational as role models for ature behavior. The angelic goodness of Eva St. Clare is the best example of Stowe's ideal, with Mrs. Shelby, Eliza, and Tom's wife Chloe also exhibiting inspiring female qualities. And though men for the most part are morally corrupt or ambivalent in *Uncle Tom's Cabin*, those who embrace so-called "feminine" values also have strong female role models: Tom, in his wife and Eva, and George Shelby, in his mother.

Religion

Finally, does *Uncle Tom's Cabin* have any sort of religious message? At first it might not seem to, especially since the two most devout characters—Eva and Tom—suffer untimely deaths. But maybe these deaths in themselves are supposed to tell us something. The reasons for Eva's illness are never fully explained, but we do know that the sights and stories of slavery's atrocity sink into her heart. Goodness and purity like Eva's cannot survive in a corrupt and evil environment, like her father's slave plantation. "I can understand why Jesus wanted to die for us.... I would die for them, Tom, if I could," she tells her friend on her deathbed. Tom also serves as a sort of "sacrificial lamb," a man who, despite preaching that "the truth will set us free," dies in captivity. And yet his miserable death affects George Shelby strongly enough to release all of his slaves from their bondage. It appears, then, that Eva and Tom serve as

Christ figures in *Uncle Tom's Cabin*, and even in the broader context of 19th century America—where their deaths evoked strong sympathy for the abolitionist cause, and moved the country that much closer to civil war.

Popularity and Reception

Uncle Tom's Cabin; or, Life Among The Lowly, to use the original subtitle, began appearing as a serial in a magazine called *National Era* on June 5, 1851; missing only two weekly installments, Stowe finished her story on April 1, 1852, making $300 for her efforts. By October 30, 1851, fan mail started flooding in, along with suggestions that the series be published in book form. At first, Stowe was skeptical about such an endeavor, as were most publishers. "I hope it will make enough so that I may have a silk dress," she modestly proclaimed.

But the book's success was immediate, promptly making a fortune for its Boston publisher and a name for Harriet Beecher Stowe. In its first year of publication, 300,000 copies of *Uncle Tom's Cabin* were sold in America and 150,000 in England. Millions of copies sold in the following years, equaling or even bettering the sales of *The Last of the Mohicans*. *Uncle Tom's Cabin* became the most popular American novel, was translated into languages from Welsh to Bangali, and inspired the praise of Leo Tolstoy, George Sand, Charles Dickens, Abraham Lincoln, and even Queen Victoria.

Nowadays, when a book or film is very popular, it is also heavily marketed; modern consumers are regularly convinced of their "need" for "101 Dalmatians" lunch boxes, "Pulp Fiction" soundtracks, and "Star Wars" action figures. In the 19th century, the craze for Uncle Tom paraphernalia was a new phenomenon. Enterprising manufacturers hurriedly produced toys, sheet music, knick knacks, and even wallpaper based on the book's plot and characters. Fans of *Uncle Tom's Cabin* eagerly purchased Uncle Tom candles, Uncle Tom teaspoons, and Uncle Tom board games, in which players raced to be the first to reunite a slave family.

And just as a best-selling novel today is often made into a movie, so *Uncle Tom's Cabin* was produced for the 19th century's equivalent to the cinema: the stage. Six months after the book's appearance, George L. Aiken's dramatic interpretation of *Uncle Tom's Cabin* opened in Troy and ran for 100 performances there, moving on to New York City for 350 shows at the National Theatre. At one time, as many as four New York companies were producing "Uncle Tom" plays simultaneously, performing up to three shows a day for packed playhouses. In the 20th century, *Uncle Tom's Cabin* continues to be reinterpreted for both stage and screen. The book's themes and characters are sometimes even incorporated into other performances; perhaps the most famous

example is Roger and Hammerstein's 1951 musical, "The King and I," in which the king's slaves present their own performance of "Uncle Tom's Cabin" in hopes of changing their master's behavior.

Despite its popularity, *Uncle Tom's Cabin* has also received its share of criticism. Southern readers have been angered by what they see as inaccuracies in the text; for example, one critic noted that Stowe always cast black characters in a better light than white characters, and that her portrayal of cruel southern slave owners was not based on fact or experience. Even more objective literary critics recognized many faults in *Uncle Tom's Cabin*, especially in its melodramatic style and pedantic tone. "As one reads the book now," said the American writer William Dean Howells in 1879, "it seems less a work of art than of spirit." In this century, questions have been raised about the novel's destructive legacy in American letters and life, and about the limitations of Stowe's liberalism. Is Stowe responsible for creating the negative "Uncle Tom" stereotype all African-Americans have had to confront, despite her good intentions? Speaking of which—just how good were her intentions, anyway? After all, she never fully allied herself with the radical abolitionist movement.

Other critics have since pointed out that racist novels written after *Uncle Tom's Cabin* did much more to establish the current Tom stereotype than Stowe's book; additionally, though Stowe's anti-slavery arguments seem cautious and naive today, they should be understood within the context of her time. But there are still no critical conclusions and no consensus concerning Stowe, her novel, her politics, and her purpose. The lively and distinguished debates concerning these issues continue to this day, ensuring that *Uncle Tom's Cabin* remains "an open book."

Study Questions

•What do you think is the significance of the black characters' lack of last names?

•What do you think of Stowe's use of the Eliza subplot? Does it help you to understand or further appreciate Tom's story, or is it simply distracting?

•When the writer George Sand reviewed *Uncle Tom's Cabin*, she noted that "children are the true heroes of Mrs. Stowe's works." Do you agree? To which children do you think she was referring?

•The scene in which George Shelby punches Simon Legree because he has just murdered Tom has been called a "shocking anticlimax." Do you think Shelby's blow is an appropriate gesture at this time? Why—and if not, how might you rewrite this part of the story?

•If Stowe was making a plea for non-violence, why are there so many violent scenes in *Uncle Tom's Cabin*? Think of three times that physical force is used in the book, and explain why you think these scenes may in fact contribute to a message of pacifism.

•Consider the strength and character of three women *and* three men in *Uncle Tom's Cabin*. Is Stowe's idea of the power of women hopelessly outdated? Why or why not?

•Why were the plot and characters of *Uncle Tom's Cabin* so intriguing to Stowe's original readers? Can you come up with three reasons why the book remains interesting to audiences today? What do the differences in your two sets of reasons say about the differences between 19th and 20th century readers of the book?

About the Essayist:

A doctoral candidate and Presidential Fellow of Columbia University, Karen Karbiener holds an MPhil from Columbia and an MA from Bryn Mawr College. She is currently an instructor in the Department of English at Columbia.